Fossil River Adventure

Mike Graf

Illustrated by Barbara Kelley

Rigby

Contents

Prologue

A river cuts a path through a wide, flat valley. Tropical sunshine warms the hot, humid forest.

Suddenly, the ground starts to vibrate. A *Stegosaurus* walks toward the edge of the river and looks for signs of danger. It splashes in the river and reaches a large sandbar.

Dark clouds gather and turn the sky gray. Lightning flashes, followed by a distant rumble of thunder.

As the rain begins to fall, a hungry *Allosaurus* thrashes through the forest, looking for a meal. When the *Allosaurus* reaches the edge of the river, it sees the *Stegosaurus* standing on the sandbar. The patter of rain turns to a heavy downpour. In spite of the storm, the *Allosaurus* tromps toward the *Stegosaurus* and opens its mouth wide. It roars, baring its sharp teeth. "Awrr!" it bellows before snapping through several of the *Stegosaurus'* plates. The *Stegosaurus* twists around and slaps its sharp tail spikes against the *Allosaurus*, knocking one of its teeth loose.

The enraged *Allosaurus* chomps on the *Stegosaurus'* neck. Although injured, the *Stegosaurus* manages to break free, but loses its balance and is swept down the river by the fast-moving water.

Zap! Lightning strikes the head of the twenty-foot *Allosaurus.* It topples over and is swept into the current. It slams against the *Stegosaurus,* which is caught against a pile of rocks, and the huge animals are whisked downstream.

The river has turned into a large, muddy lake. And at the bottom of this lake lie the bodies of two large dinosaurs.

Chapter 1

A Family Trip

"*Let's go hiking, hiking, hiking. Let's go hiking by the stream. Let's go hiking—*"

Mr. Chang stopped singing and glanced at the passengers in the car. "Come on! I don't want to be the only one singing!"

"*Let's go hiking, hiking, hiking!*" the rest of his family chimed in. "*Let's go hiking by the stream!*"

Terrence checked his loose tooth with his tongue as he sang along, "*Leth go hiking, hiking, hiking. Leth go hiking by the thream!*"

"Terrence, are you playing with your loose tooth again?" his mother asked after hearing his slurred words.

"I'm checking to make sure my tooth is still there!" Terrence replied.

"What a great voice!" his father joked.

Terrence's seven-year-old sister Kristy imitated her brother, "*Leth go hiking, hiking, hiking. Leth go hiking by the thream!*" She burst into laughter.

Mr. Chang suddenly announced, "Hey, look everyone. There's a dinosaur ahead."

Terrence quickly leaned forward in the backseat and shouted, "Where?"

His father pointed out the front windshield. "Just ahead. Right next to the road. See it?" Mr. Chang slowed the car as they approached a gigantic green dinosaur that stood at the edge of the highway.

"Is it real?" Kristy asked.

"Honey, it's just a model of a dinosaur," Mrs. Chang answered.

"Not just *any* dinosaur. It's an *Apatosaurus!*" Terrence shouted as they pulled up next to it. "There's no need to fear, though. It's a herbivore, so it eats only plants."

Mrs. Chang looked back at her son. "Terrence, I'm always amazed at how much you know about dinosaurs."

"It's because he's always reading," Kristy said, grabbing Terrence's *Dinosaurs of the Jurassic Period* book from his lap and holding it up.

"Mom, you know I love dinosaurs," Terrence said.

This year, Terrence had participated in his school's annual science fair. He had hoped to win first prize, but the judges said that his dinosaur fossil display "needed to be more realistic." He was so disappointed when he didn't win that he vowed never to participate again. But his dad encouraged him to continue to work on his project and to enter it in the science fair again next year. One of the reasons his parents decided to take this trip was to give Terrence a chance to do some firsthand dinosaur research. Terrence still wasn't sure about entering the science fair again, but he was very happy to be taking this trip. This was his chance to see real dinosaur fossils.

Mr. Chang rolled down the window. The dinosaur had a welcoming smile painted on its face. At the base of the dinosaur was a sign that read "Welcome to Fossil River National Park."

"Can we take a picture, Daddy?" Kristy called out.

"Sure," Mr. Chang answered.

The family got out of the car and Mr. Chang, Terrence, and Kristy assembled in front of the dinosaur.

Mrs. Chang stayed back and set the camera on the hood of the car. She leaned over and peered through the lens. "Move a bit to the left, everyone. I want to get all of you *and* the dinosaur's face."

"*Apatosauruses* were huge, Mom. They were over 70 feet long and 40 feet tall," Terrence called back to her.

"You'd need a panoramic camera to get all of him," Mr. Chang observed.

"Well, our ancient camera will have to do for now." Mrs. Chang pushed a button to set the automatic timer. She ran over to join her family. "Say 'dinosaur.'"

"Dinosaur!" everyone shouted. The camera clicked.

Terrence turned around and shielded his eyes with his hand as he looked up at the giant man-made *Apatosaurus.* Its belly arched far above Terrence's head.

Kristy wrapped her arms around one of the dinosaur's massive legs. She tried to touch the fingers of each hand together as she reached around the leg, but they didn't even come close. "He's huge!" she exclaimed. "Too bad you didn't have him for your science project, Terrence."

Mr. Chang smiled, then reminded his family, "We better get going. It's 7:30 already and we still have at least a five-mile drive to the campground. The ranger talk starts at 8:00. Let's go to that so we can learn about the park."

The Changs returned to their car and headed down the highway. The road followed a broad, winding river.

"It sure is quiet out here," Mrs. Chang said.

The road took a sharp bend and climbed a series of small hills.

Terrence looked out the back window and gazed at the green grass and cottonwood trees that lined the river. When Terrence looked in front of him, he saw the sandy hills of the desert and a few scattered plants and small trees. He tried to imagine dinosaurs walking over this land millions of years ago.

Finally, Mr. Chang turned off the highway and stopped at the entrance to Fossil River National Park. At the tollbooth, he paid the entrance fee and received a park brochure. He handed the brochure back to Terrence and drove in.

At the top of a steep hill, Mr. Chang suddenly braked.

"Wow!" the Changs cried in unison.

The abrupt stop caught Terrence by surprise. He had been wiggling his loose tooth and it popped out onto his tongue. He fished through his mouth with his finger and pulled it out. Terrence slipped the tooth into his pants pocket as his father pulled to the side of the road.

"Let's get out and take a look," Mr. Chang exclaimed as he shut off the engine.

Terrence peered through the front window at a huge, oddly shaped mountain. Then he hopped out of the car with the brochure in his hand.

The Changs walked over to a viewing area and gazed at the mountain. It poked straight up as if it was squeezed right out of the ground. Near the top of the mountain, strangely shaped rocks stuck out in all directions.

"I've never seen such an unusual-looking mountain," Mrs. Chang remarked.

"It's called Split Mountain," Terrence announced, looking up from the park brochure. "When the mountain pushed up out of the ground, it started to crack and that's where the river came through and split it in half."

"That must be the same river we passed a few miles ago," Mr. Chang added.

"Yes, that's Fossil River and it winds through the entire park." Terrence smiled as he held up the brochure. "This brochure has lots of cool stuff in it."

The family watched silently as the sun got lower in the western sky. As it did, the mountain seemed to slowly change color from orange to red to purple, and then faded to a soft pink glow.

Kristy said, "That's pretty!"

"I could watch this forever," Mr. Chang added.

"I could, too. But we better get to that ranger program," Mrs. Chang reminded her family.

The Changs climbed back into the car and drove to the campground's outdoor theater.

Chapter 2

Fossil River National Park

Mr. Chang parked the car at the outdoor theater parking lot and everyone hopped out. The Changs quietly found seats in the back row just as a ranger walked onto the stage.

"Good evening. My name is Rich, and I've worked here at Fossil River National Park for over ten years. I'm one of the park's paleontologists. We study fossils, which are the remains of plants and animals from long ago. At this park, we study the fossils of a particular type of animal."

Terrence leaned forward in anticipation.

"Fossil River National Park is famous for dinosaur fossils," Rich said. "Dinosaurs were land-dwelling reptiles that lived long ago. I studied dinosaurs in college. Dinosaurs are just about the most interesting animals that ever lived. I'm fascinated by them, so that's why I'm here—and I'm sure that's why many of you are here, too." He smiled.

Sure is, thought Terrence.

"The dinosaur bones in this area were first discovered in 1906, after a heavy rainstorm. Two people were out walking and came upon a skull and some teeth. The fossils were visible because the storm had washed away lots of soil. It was a 'lucky strike'—by that we mean it was an easy and un-expected discovery."

While Rich walked over to turn on a slide projector, he explained, "Those first fossils belonged to the park's most common dinosaur, the *Apatosaurus,* which used to be called the *Brontosaurus.*" He carried the remote control back to the podium and clicked on a projector. A picture of a huge dinosaur appeared on a large screen above the stage.

The audience laughed when they recognized the green statue at the entrance to the park.

"I see that you've met Anna the *Apatosaurus,* our park mascot," Rich smiled. "The *Apatosaurus* was a herbivore. It was one of the largest land animals that ever lived. The *Apatosaurus,* along with the other dinosaurs found here, lived during the Jurassic Period, which was over 145 million years ago."

"See, I told you it was a herbivore," Terrence boasted to Kristy.

Kristy gave her brother a small poke in response.

Rich clicked the projector. "This is a *Stegosaurus.* It was also a herbivore. It had rows of large plates down its back that looked like fan blades. Notice the 2-foot-long, sharp spikes on its tail. You wouldn't want to be whacked by one of those!"

Rich flipped to the next slide. "Here's an

Stegosaurus

Allosaurus. The *Allosaurus* was one of the most ferocious carnivores, or meat-eaters, that ever lived. The *Allosaurus* dined on herbivores, such as the *Apatosaurus* and *Stegosaurus.* It looked for young, old, or weak animals because none of these dinosaurs were easy to capture. The *Allosaurus* really had to battle for

Allosaurus

its meals. It was also constantly fighting other *Allosauruses* over territory and mates.

"There are many different types of dinosaur fossils that we've discovered here at the park as well," Rich continued. "We've found footprints, tooth marks, eggs, and animal waste that were left behind by the dinosaurs. These fossils help us figure out how dinosaurs lived." Rich showed a slide of huge animal footprints.

"Dinosaur teeth and bones can also become fossils. These fossils are created when a dinosaur dies and is quickly buried in sand or mud. Except for the teeth and bones, the rest of the body rots away."

The next slide showed a picture of several fossilized bones.

"Ever since the first *Apatosaurus, Stegosaurus,* and *Allosaurus* fossils were found in this park, paleontologists have continued to search for more," Rich continued.

Terrence shivered with excitement. He closed his eyes and tried to imagine what it would be like if dinosaurs still wandered around the park. Terrence imagined a large *Allosaurus* searching along the river for prey. The bright light of the next slide made Terrence open his eyes.

On the screen was a photograph of two teeth. Rich

pointed to one of them. "This fossilized tooth is from a herbivore. It's about 3 inches long and shaped like an unsharpened pencil." He pointed to the other tooth. "This sharp, 3-inch-long tooth was from an *Allosaurus.* The tooth has tiny bumps along the edges like a saw blade to cut and tear meat."

Terrence slipped his hand into his pocket and felt his tooth. He touched its edges and wondered if he was meant to be a herbivore or carnivore. Just then, his stomach growled. He pulled his hand from his pocket and sat up to listen.

"So far, there are over 400 places in this park where we have found fossils of teeth, bones, and footprints. We are constantly discovering new sites. Most sites are not open to the public, but there are a few you can visit."

Rich brought up the last slide. "One of the most famous sites in the park is the dinosaur quarry, where thousands of dinosaur bones are still being excavated. I'll be leading tours through the quarry tomorrow morning starting at 9:00. I hope to see you there."

Rich shut off the slide projector, and the audience clapped.

Mr. Chang looked at Terrence. "I bet I know where you want to go tomorrow!"

Chapter 3

The Dinosaur Quarry

The Changs joined dozens of other people at the Visitor Center the next morning for a tour of the dinosaur quarry. Rich, the ranger who had spoken at the campfire talk the night before, led them to where part of a hillside was cut out.

As Rich walked the group through the excavation site, he explained, "This is one of the largest active dinosaur quarries in the world. Over 1,600 dinosaur bones are visible here." Rich stopped and pointed to the group of bones embedded in the hillside.

"Look right here," Rich said, pointing to the middle of the hill. "We have bones from several dinosaurs all in one place. They most likely lived in the same area."

The group followed Rich farther into the quarry. "Over here, we have some complete fossils. This whole string of bones makes up the complete tail of a *Stegosaurus*."

When the group was near the edge of the hill, Terrence stopped and looked back at all the fossils that were scattered throughout the hillside. He ran to catch up to the group, then asked Rich, "Why did you leave all these bones here? Don't you want to dig them up and put them back together?"

Rich smiled. "I'm glad you asked that. Originally, we tried to remove as many of the bones as we could. But we've left the rest here for one reason. We want visitors like you to be able to see them."

Near the end of the quarry, Terrence noticed a 5-foot-long leg bone embedded in the hillside. It had a sign next to it.

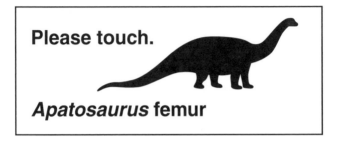

Please touch.

Apatosaurus **femur**

Mrs. Chang pulled out her camera. "Kristy and Terrence, stand next to that sign so I can get a picture. Smile!" Mrs. Chang called out, then snapped the photo.

Terrence ran his hand over the femur. He noticed several sharp grooves near the end of the bone.

Rich came over to Terrence. "Aren't those interesting marks? We think they were made by an *Allosaurus* that was gnawing on the bone."

Terrence replied, "I sure would have liked to have seen that!"

"I know what you mean," Rich answered. He turned and spoke to the entire group. "I want to let everyone know that we just discovered a place in the park where several dinosaur skulls are being excavated.

That site is less than a half-mile away from here, and a guided walk to that location starts in a few minutes."

Terrence looked at his parents.

"I know what you're thinking," Mr. Chang smiled.

"Of course we can go," Mrs. Chang added. "That's what we're here for."

The Changs stepped outside and waited with a group of others for the tour to see the skulls. A woman walked up and greeted them. She carried a yellow helmet and wore beige overalls and kneepads. Hanging from her belt were several tools that rattled and clanked when she walked.

"I wonder what she's going to fix with those tools," Kristy whispered.

"Nothing. She's a paleontologist," Terrence explained. "She uses those tools to find fossils."

"Hello. My name's Allison, and I'm leading the walk this morning," the woman announced. "I'll be taking you to one of the most amazing sites we've ever discovered in this park. We're cutting into the hillside where there's some loose rock and dirt. That's why I'm bringing this helmet. I'll be staying up there to participate in the dig after I show it to you."

Allison slipped on her backpack. "Follow me." She led the group of visitors on a faint path that sloped gently up a hill. "This whole area used to be flat and covered by the ocean. Dinosaurs were buried in the sand and mud at the bottom of that ocean," she said.

Allison stopped to let the group catch up, and then added, "As we head farther up this hill, we're going about 145 million years back in time."

Kristy's eyes opened wide. "Are we going to see real live dinosaurs?"

Allison heard her and smiled. "No. Dinosaurs lived a long time ago. I meant that when we get to the top of this hill, we'll be standing on very old soil. It's much older than the soil at the bottom of the hill."

Terrence thought for a second, then asked, "Wouldn't the oldest layer be at the bottom?"

Allison looked out at the group. "I bet most of you are wondering why the soil is older up here. Let me explain." She set down her backpack. "Over many years, the ground lifted up to form mountains. So, the sand and mud from the bottom of the ocean covered the top of the new mountains. Then, over millions of years, the newer top layers of soil washed down the sides of the mountains. What is left up here is the old soil with the dinosaur bones."

"Dinosaur bones?" Terrence blurted out. "Right here at our feet?"

"That's right." Allison reached down and scooped up a handful of the reddish clay dirt. "This is the soil layer that we are finding dinosaur bones in." She pointed down the hill. "If you look down there, you'll see that the newer soil is sandy colored. We haven't found any dinosaurs in that layer at all. So now you all know where to look for dinosaur bones around here.

"We paleontologists like to call erosion our 'best friend.' That's because it washes away topsoil and shows us the fossils that are underneath. Let's go meet a fossil." Allison slung on her backpack and turned to walk ahead, then paused. "His nickname is 'Cheese,' and he's very fragile. So, please, no touching."

The group followed Allison to the top of the hill, where a section of the ground was dug out. The area was marked with a stake that had a red ribbon on it. "This is the dinosaur site, and as you can see, there is a dig going on." There were many tools scattered around and several buckets filled with what looked like chunks of rock.

Allison grabbed a rock from the bucket and held it up. "This looks like a rock, but it actually has a fossilized bone in it. We think it's part of a leg bone. Take a close look, and then pass it around." She handed the rock to a visitor, then pulled out three smaller rocks, which she pieced together. "These bones are part of a rib, probably from a baby

Stegosaurus." She passed the three rib fossils to Mr. Chang.

"Amazing," Mr. Chang said. "At first glance, they look like ordinary rocks. But they definitely fit together like a rib." He passed the bones on to Terrence.

Mrs. Chang pulled out her camera. "Don't move, Terrence. I want to get a picture of you holding the rib fossils." She held the camera up. "Hold the bones in place," she instructed.

"Oh, Mom, not again," Terrence said, but he put the bones together as Mrs. Chang snapped a picture.

Allison introduced some paleontologists who were busy digging. "Sue and Randy are working to get fossils out of the ground, including the skull that we call 'Cheese.'"

Allison traced the outline of a skull in the middle of a rock. "Let me help you see it," Allison said as she dusted off Cheese's face with a paintbrush.

"Cheese looks like he's smiling," Kristy exclaimed.

"Exactly," Allison said. "He's saying 'cheese' and baring his teeth for all the visitors who take pictures. It's rare to find a skull like this with so many teeth in place. We're not sure what type of dinosaur Cheese was. It might be a dinosaur we haven't discovered yet. After we get the skull out, we'll try to identify it."

For a few minutes, the group watched the paleontologists digging around the base of the rock that contained the skull.

Allison spoke to the group. "When you visit other areas of the park, feel free to walk around and keep your eyes open for fossils. If you find something interesting, leave it where you found it and come tell us. We're very interested in discovering what else is out there."

Terrence looked at his parents. "I want to go exploring."

Chapter 4

Exploring Indian Creek Trail

The Changs pulled into an empty parking lot while Terrence glanced at the park map. "This is where Indian Creek Trail is," he announced.

"Let's just hike around and see what's out here, just like Allison suggested," Mrs. Chang said. "There's no one else around. It'll be fun to have the whole place to ourselves."

The Changs climbed out of the car. Mr. Chang pulled his backpack from the trunk. "I'm bringing snacks. Maybe we'll find a nice sunny spot somewhere next to the creek to eat."

Terrence led his family up the canyon on a faint trail that followed a stream.

Terrence stopped and looked at the streambed while he waited for his family to catch up.

"There's barely a trickle of water in it," Mrs. Chang said.

Kristy bent down and picked up a small rock by

the edge of the stream. "Look at this! It's a fossil."

"It's a seashell fossil," Terrence said. "I have a bunch of these at home."

"I think it might be a clam fossil," Mrs. Chang said.

"Can I keep it?" Kristy asked. "I want to start a fossil collection like Terrence has."

Mr. Chang shook his head. "Terrence got his fossils from a museum gift shop and from private land. We can't take anything from the park."

"Who would know?" Kristy asked.

"We would," Mrs. Chang replied. "Just think how this park would look if everyone took a fossil home for a souvenir."

"OK," Kristy sighed, setting the clam fossil back where she found it.

Mr. Chang looked around. "There are the red bands of dirt. We're hiking in the same soil that dinosaur bones are found in. Maybe we'll be lucky and find a fossil. Let's look around carefully while we hike."

Terrence stepped off the path and bent down to look at a colorful rock that was wedged in the ground. He quickly dug out the rock and held it up. "A rainbow rock!" Terrence called out.

Mrs. Chang stood next to Terrence. "May I see it?"

He handed the rock to his mom. She scratched her fingernail against it. "It's quite hard, but I don't think it's a dinosaur bone." Terrence put the rock back.

They continued looking for fossils. Terrence picked up another rock and inspected it, then another and another. None of the rocks seemed to have bones, teeth, or impressions of footprints in them. "It's not as easy as looking for seashell fossils in the hills near our house," Terrence announced impatiently. "Seashell fossils are all over the place.

"I don't know how you can tell which rocks have fossils, and which ones don't," Terrence continued as he held up a small stone. "They're all starting to look the same to me."

"Let's keep heading up the trail," Mrs. Chang suggested. "Maybe we'll find a better place to look."

"If we last that long," Mr. Chang said, taking off his hat and wiping his forehead with a bandanna. "It sure is hot and humid out here."

Terrence sat down on a large boulder and tilted his head back to guzzle water from his water bottle. He stared at the sky. Clouds were swelling up and changing shape before his eyes. "Look up, you guys!"

Mrs. Chang looked up. "We better look for shelter. It looks like a storm's coming."

Terrence got up and forged ahead while his family

followed. The trail hugged a small cliff above the streambed in the deep canyon.

Terrence took a few steps uphill to get a better look at more rocks. As he climbed, loose dirt kicked out underneath him, sending down a small avalanche. Terrence lifted his foot out of the hole he created. "This soil is really soft," Terrence announced as he slowly slid back down the hill.

His father looked at the pile of dirt and rocks that Terrence had knocked loose. "I guess people can cause hillsides to erode, too. Maybe we better stay on the trail."

Terrence continued to survey the landscape as they hiked. "We're in a rock junkyard," he said. "There are rocks everywhere."

A small breeze kicked up, blowing bits of dust across the trail. The dust began blowing around until a dust devil formed, swirling the trail dirt in a small spiral. The miniature twister picked up more dust and bounced this way and that across the path in front of them.

As the dust devil twirled closer, Terrence held his hat down on his head. "Close your eyes!" he warned. The dust devil whisked across the trail ahead of the family, then lost strength as it climbed a small side canyon. Hoping to get ahead of it, the Changs scurried farther up the trail. As soon as they did, the dust devil seemed to change its mind. It spun right back toward Terrence and his family.

"Duck!" Mr. Chang called out as sand blew across his face.

The family covered their eyes as the dust devil spun by. It threw sand and small rocks into the air, and swept Terrence's hat right off his head.

As soon as the windstorm passed, Terrence poked his head up and opened his eyes. He and his family stood up and looked around. The dust devil twirled downstream, skipping back and forth along the trail that they had hiked up.

Terrence saw his hat caught in the branches of a bush on the other side of the stream. "I'll be right back." He climbed down a small cliff and stepped into the water. His foot immediately squished into thick, gooey mud that coated the bottom of the streambed. With each step, his feet sank into the ground with a slurping sound. When he finally got across the stream, Terrence grabbed his hat, put it back on his head, and turned around to walk back. Just as he was about to take a step, Terrence looked to the left and froze. "Mom! Dad! Kristy! You have to see this!"

Chapter 5

The Storm

Mr. and Mrs. Chang and Kristy ran down to Terrence. About 10 feet away from him lay the skeleton of a large animal.

Kristy hid behind her mother and peeked around her legs. "What is it?"

"You mean, what *was* it," Terrence replied.

"A bighorn sheep," Mrs. Chang answered.

"Its horns are huge!" Terrence exclaimed.

"Do you think it will become a fossil?" Kristy asked.

"Only if it gets buried quickly in the dirt," Terrence reminded her.

"There's hardly any meat left on those bones," Mr. Chang said. "The scavengers must have been working on it for quite a while." He looked up and saw several vultures circling under a dark gray mass of clouds. The air was cooler and the breeze picked up. "Come on, let's keep going."

The Changs climbed back toward the trail. At the top of the hill, Terrence paused and glanced back at the sheep skeleton, then looked at the sky. Lightning flashed in the distance, followed by a soft rumble of thunder.

"Let's head over to those rocks and take shelter," Mr. Chang said. "I don't think we'll have time to get back to the car before the rain starts."

Terrence caught up to his family. He glanced back at the hill and noticed a large stake with a red ribbon tied to it. He remembered that was the dig site where they'd met "Cheese" earlier.

"Terrence!" his father called out. "Hurry up!"

"Coming!" Terrence said as he ran.

"Smell the air," Mrs. Chang said. "It's going to rain for sure."

There was another rumble of thunder. The family hurried toward some overhanging rocks.

Terrence felt a drop of rain on his nose. "Rain! I felt rain!" he called out excitedly.

Kristy looked up at the sky, tilted her head, and opened her mouth to catch a raindrop. "Got one!" she cried.

More raindrops pattered down and pelted against the dry, dusty soil as Mr. Chang led his family to a cavelike hole in the rock. "Hopefully the storm won't last too long."

The sky blinked with a flash of light and the

thunder boomed. "The lightning's closer," Mrs. Chang announced, peering up at the sky.

It was pouring now. The Changs huddled together in a circle. Mr. Chang slipped off his backpack and pulled out a picnic blanket. The family draped it over their heads like a small tent. Terrence found a few sticks and propped them up under the blanket. Their makeshift tent offered extra protection from the rain.

The family squeezed closer together.

They ate granola bars and apples while the rain pounded the ground all around. *Zap!* Lightning lit up the sky nearby. *Kaboom!* Thunder shook the whole area.

"One, two, three, four. I counted to four. The lighting is less than a mile away," Terrence stated.

Mrs. Chang smiled at her son.

The rain fell with a constant, loud roar. It was hard to hear one another talk. The Changs sat quietly in their shelter and watched the ground become drenched. It was as if a giant hose had been turned on in the sky.

"It's really getting muddy out there," Mr. Chang realized. "I'm going to take a quick look around."

"Don't go out in the open," Mrs. Chang said. "It's not the right place to be during a thunderstorm."

Mr. Chang slipped out from under the blanket

and walked a few feet away from their shelter. He held his hands above his head and squinted his eyes. The downpour instantly soaked him. He looked toward the stream. The small stream was now a river of fast-moving, muddy water.

Mr. Chang hurried back under the blanket with his family. He took off his hat and shook off some of the rainwater. "The stream is getting high. But I think it's best to wait out the storm here and try to stay as dry as we can." He shivered and rubbed his upper arms. "It sure got cold fast!"

"It was so calm this morning," Mrs. Chang recalled. "It's hard to believe how quickly the weather changed. I didn't even think to bring raingear on our hike. At least we have hats on," she said. "This blanket is soaked."

Kristy looked up and a drop plunked on her nose. "Are we going to sleep out here?"

Mr. Chang glanced at his watch. "I don't think so. It's only 7:00 now. Once the storm lets up, we should have plenty of time to hike back to our car and drive back to camp before dark. I have a flashlight in my backpack if we need it."

"I wonder how high the water is now. I haven't heard thunder in a while." Terrence lifted the edge of the blanket and checked. "The stream is full of water and moving fast," he announced. "And water's sloshing down all the hills, too." He pulled his head under the blanket and looked at his family. "Do you think that bighorn sheep will get washed away?"

"With this storm, it's probably way downstream by now," Mrs. Chang replied.

The rain turned to a roar. Water splashed up inside their makeshift tent.

"Yikes! I'm getting soaked!" Terrence called out.

Kristy peeked out from a corner of the blanket. "Hey! Little white balls are falling from the sky."

"That's hail," Terrence told his sister, looking out.

At first, a few hailstones were mixed in with the rain. Soon, hundreds of small balls of ice were pounding against the blanket and bouncing up from the dirt like miniature ping-pong balls. Afraid of being struck by one of the balls of ice, Kristy and Terrence huddled in closer to their parents. The storm roared outside.

Mrs. Chang started singing to try to drown out the noise of the hail. "*It's raining, it's pouring . . .* " She looked around at her family. "Sing with me!"

The family joined in, "*It's raining, it's pouring . . .*"

Soon, the hail let up and the ground was covered with marble-sized balls of white ice. From where the Changs sat, they could see that the water had risen to the top of the streambed. Rapid, muddy water churned along, creating whitecaps on the water. Small branches from bushes were being swept downstream. Rain continued to pound down.

Lightning flashed again. The family counted together, "One, two, three, four, five, six, seven, eight." Then there was a soft rumble of thunder.

"It's farther away now," Terrence observed.

"I think the rain is letting up, too," Mr. Chang said. "I'll go out and check the stream. Hopefully, we can head back to the car soon."

"Can I go with you, Dad?" Terrence asked.

"Yes, but be very careful," Mr. Chang responded.

Terrence climbed out first. Hunched over, he crawled out from the dripping wet blanket and headed toward a grove of trees. When he reached the outer edge of the grove, he stood up and looked at the wide, murky stream that was racing by with a roar just inches from his feet. Terrence shielded his eyes from the rain, turned around, and shouted back to his dad. "This looks just like the Colorado River!"

"Terrence, please stay away from the edge," his dad called.

As he spoke, a portion of the riverbank broke away under Terrence's feet. "Dad!" he screamed as he fell into the water.

"Terrence!" Mr. Chang hollered. Mrs. Chang heard them, threw off the blanket, and was instantly at her husband's side, holding on to Kristy's hand tightly. They watched, horrified, as the current swept Terrence away from them.

Mr. Chang took off after Terrence, with his wife and Kristy close behind.

Chapter 6

Flash Flood

Mr. and Mrs. Chang and Kristy ran along the banks of the swollen stream, trying to keep up with Terrence. The stream had turned into a river of fast, muddy water that flooded over the banks and covered parts of the trail. Plants and small trees that the floodwaters had uprooted raced by. The Changs scrambled through brush and hopped over muddy puddles as they tried to catch Terrence.

Terrence was pulled downstream in the current. "Help!" he screamed just as his head dipped below water. A few seconds later, his head bobbed back up. Terrence was pulled around a bend in the stream and grabbed onto a large rock. His parents saw him struggling as they stood on the trail above the stream.

"Terrence!" they called.

"Here!" he managed to yell.

The current swept Terrence from the safety of the large rock and pushed him downstream. There, he was able to grab on to a large, leafy bush that was sticking out of the water.

Terrence twisted his body around in the water and tightly held several thick branches. He steadied himself while facing downstream. He put his legs against the bush and inched them down toward the bottom. He held still for a second until his feet found the base of the plant. Terrence placed his feet as low as he could and pushed himself toward the shore.

The Changs saw their son and ran toward him.

A side stream was raging by and had washed out the faint trail that led to where Terrence was stranded.

"We'll have to find a place to jump across!" Mr. Chang called out.

Mrs. Chang looked down at Kristy, who shivered at her side. "Are you OK?" she asked her daughter.

"I'm cold!" Kristy replied.

Mr. Chang gazed ahead and saw Terrence groping toward the shore.

"It looks like he's going to make it to shore," Mr. Chang said.

Mr. and Mrs. Chang found a narrow place to cross the side stream so they could get back on the trail. The muddy soil was thick and gooey and covered their shoes, making their steps heavy and slow.

"Give me your hand," Mr. Chang coaxed Kristy, then lifted her to where he was standing.

Mrs. Chang followed right behind them.

"There!" Mrs. Chang called out, pointing at the raging stream. "I think we'll be able to get across over there," she cried.

Mr. Chang walked over to the narrow area and jumped. Then he reached for Kristy to help her across.

"Careful!" Mrs. Chang said while holding on to Kristy from the other side.

Kristy reached out as far as she could and grabbed her father's hand. Mr. Chang hoisted her safely across.

Suddenly, the ground next to the stream gave out underneath Mr. Chang, and he plunked straight into the water. He grabbed on to the shore and pulled himself out of the water as Mrs. Chang jumped across the stream.

Terrence continued sloshing through the shallow water toward dry land. With shaking legs, he walked farther out of the water. His soaked clothes hung heavily on his shivering body. Terrence staggered as he walked.

Terrence lost his balance and dropped to his knees. "I'm cold," he moaned. "I'm so cold." Terrence struggled the last few feet to shore then collapsed onto the muddy ground.

Chapter 7

Safe!

"Are you OK?" an unfamiliar voice asked.

Terrence lifted his head and squinted his eyes. "I don't know," he whispered. He rolled onto his stomach. His face was coated with mud and cool water lapped at his feet.

"Do you know what happened?" the voice asked.

Terrence slowly lifted his head. "I was standing next to the stream and the ground just gave away, and the next thing I knew I was in the water."

Another person bent down next to Terrence. "You did a pretty good job of pulling yourself out of the stream."

The Changs quickly stepped up to hug Terrence.

"You had us so worried," Mrs. Chang sighed with relief as she squeezed her son.

"I guess I should have been more careful," Terrence said.

Terrence looked up at one of the strangers who surrounded him and said, "You were at the dinosaur quarry this morning. You're the one who taught the campfire program last night, right?"

"Yes. I'm Rich. Allison is here, too. Do you remember her?"

Terrence nodded and shivered as he looked down at his wet, muddy clothes. He felt his head and said, "I lost my hat."

"It's probably way downstream by now. You should get that wet shirt off, Terrence. Here, I have a blanket for you," Rich said.

Terrence sat down, took off his shirt, and wrapped himself in the warm blanket.

The ranger took off his jacket and slipped it over Terrence's shoulders. "That's quite a journey you took," Rich concluded. "In another half mile, you would have been dropped into Fossil River, which is over a half-mile wide after a storm like this. You might not have gotten out of there. You are one lucky young man, Terrence."

"I guess so." Terrence pulled the blanket and jacket tightly around his body and tried to stop shaking.

"How did you know we were here?" Mr. Chang asked Rich.

"We were doing a sweep of the parking lot before we shut the gate for the night. Then we saw your car still parked there. Since it was so late in the day, we started searching for the owners. So here we are." Rich glanced at Terrence. "You *are* OK, aren't you?"

Terrence thought about the question. He remembered being helplessly dropped into the stream, being pulled underwater, grabbing onto the bush, then pushing himself out. He also remembered his father's words of caution and wished he had taken his warning a little more seriously. "I think I'm OK," Terrence finally replied.

"We'd better get you back to the campsite and into some dry clothes," Mrs. Chang said. "Do you think you can walk back?"

"I'm fine," Terrence assured her. He started to get up, moving carefully to make sure he wasn't hurt.

"Ouch! What was that?" Terrence said as he tried to stand up. His knee had hit something hard and sharp in the mud. He moved his knee and put his hand down to see what was there. He felt a sharp stone. Terrence dug around it a bit more, then looked up at Rich.

Rich moved closer and shined his flashlight at the sand. "Whoa!" he exclaimed.

Terrence pulled the stone from the ground and cleaned it off. He held the stone up to the light.

"I can't believe it!" Rich exclaimed.

"Believe what?" Allison asked.

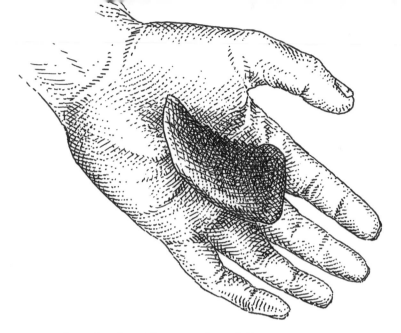

"Look what Terrence found."

Terrence held a small stone in his hand.

Mrs. Chang stepped up to take a closer look. "What is that?"

"Allison, what do you make of this?" Rich asked. Terrence gave the object to Allison.

Allison turned the sharp, black, 3-inch-long object around several times in her hands. "It looks lethal." She handed it back to Terrence. "No doubt about it, it's an *Allosaurus* tooth."

"That's what I thought!" Rich added.

"An *Allosaurus* tooth? Right here in my hand?" Terrence exclaimed.

"Right there in your hand," Allison said. "The flood must have washed the tooth down here or carried away enough soil to help unbury it," she said. "That's why we say that erosion really *is* a paleontologist's best friend."

"You mean I've discovered a real fossil?" Terrence asked in surprise. "Does that make me a real paleontologist?"

"I think you're well on your way to becoming one," Allison said. "We'll have to take this tooth back to the lab tonight for safekeeping."

Terrence handed the tooth back to Allison. She stood up, wrapped the tooth in a tissue, and carefully placed it in her backpack. "Rich and I will come back here tomorrow to search the whole area. Since you found one tooth here, there's a chance we'll find more. Would you all like to join us?"

"Sure!" Terrence replied. "Can we, Dad? Mom?"

Mr. Chang thought for a second. "What we need to do right now is to go back to camp and get you into some dry clothes."

"We can talk about it in the morning," Mrs. Chang added.

"I think that means *yes!*" Terrence called out.

"We'll see you in the morning, then," Rich said.

Chapter 8

Fossil Hunt

"Good morning! I'm glad to see all of you!" Allison greeted the Changs at the trailhead parking lot. "Isn't the weather beautiful today?"

"It's especially nice after last night's storm," Mrs. Chang agreed.

"We're glad to be here," Mr. Chang added. "We didn't want to miss the fossil hunt. Terrence and I have a rafting trip planned for this afternoon, but we can spend most of the morning here."

Allison noticed a few scratches on Terrence's face. "How are you doing today?"

"Great!" Terrence replied. "I'm ready to search."

"I'm happy to hear that. We are, too," Allison said as she grabbed a sign from the back of her truck. She walked over to the trailhead and hammered the sign into the ground. "There," she said, stepping back to read it.

CAUTION
Trail Temporarily Closed to the
Public Because of Flooding

Allison strung a chain across the trail entrance. "That ought to keep visitors away for a while," she said.

"Are you going to repair the trail where it washed out?" Mrs. Chang asked.

"We have a crew coming later to fix it," Allison answered. "We're really closing this trail because of what Terrence found. We can't have a place like this open to the public until we find out exactly what's out there."

Rich drove up in another truck and hopped out. "Hey, Terrence! I'm glad to see you up on this bright, sunny morning." He squinted up into the sunshine. "It can be like that around here. One day it rains in torrents, the next day it's clear."

Allison and Rich got shovels, picks, brushes, buckets, and a small sack of hand tools from their trucks. They threw some tools into their backpacks and passed others around to the Changs.

"Let's go back to where Terrence found that tooth last night," Allison said. "Does everyone have a snack and something to drink?"

"Yes," Mr. Chang answered, reaching around and patting his large backpack.

"This is going to be fun!" Kristy exclaimed.

Allison and Rich led Terrence and his family up

the faint trail the Changs had hiked the day before.

As they walked, Rich said, "You folks were in the biggest storm we've had out here in over ten years. We got over 2 inches of rain in less than an hour at the Visitor Center. That's a lot of rain for the desert. With everything so dry and sandy, the stream rose really quickly. We haven't had a flash flood like that in a long time."

They stopped and looked at the stream. The water was still cloudy from the flood, but it was flowing slowly and the water level was much lower.

"It's hard to believe how wild it was yesterday," Terrence said to the group. "I bet I could walk across that stream right now."

"Did you know," Allison asked, "that all the water on Earth has been around for millions of years, even before there were dinosaurs? Who knows, Terrence, maybe the water you were in last night contained some of the same drops of water that the *Allosauruses* drank."

Rich continued. "Just think, dinosaur bones and teeth are buried for millions of years. Then we have one storm like last night's and there's enough erosion for Terrence to find a dinosaur tooth. What a lucky strike!"

"Hey," Terrence recalled, "that was how they discovered the first bones in this park a hundred years ago. Right?"

"You're right, Terrence," Rich replied. "They were looking for fossils after a storm. But they had searched for years before that."

They hiked on. The hills around them rolled from one to the next, each with layers of red and gray rock in them. After rounding a bend in the path, they stopped at the top of a rise. Down below was a stake in the sand that marked the place where Terrence had found the *Allosaurus* tooth.

"I see your footprints in the sand, Terrence," Kristy observed.

"I know." Terrence dashed down the hill and started digging.

"Terrence!" Mrs. Chang called. "You should wait until Allison says its OK to dig."

"He's OK," Allison answered. "We'll be down there in a minute with our tools. Anyway, with his luck, he's likely to dig up another treasure!"

Chapter 9

Digging for Dinosaurs

Terrence dug a large hole around the stake that marked the place where he found the *Allosaurus* tooth.

"Find anything interesting?" Allison asked while walking by.

Terrence sat up and wiped his forearm over his face. "Not yet," he sighed.

Kristy sat down next to her brother and helped him dig.

"Actually, Terrence, most fossils are much harder to find than that tooth you discovered," Allison said. "Usually fossils are buried underground. But thanks to erosion, sometimes fossils can be found above the ground.

"Fossils can also look just like plain rocks," Allison added. "You have to know what to look for. Look for rocks that have a bone shape in them, or for something that looks like a piece of dried-up sponge."

"Some fossils can be really tiny," Rich continued. "We discovered a baby dinosaur site in the park recently. Some of the fossils there were barely an inch long. We've even found fossils of dinosaur eggs. Inside the eggs we found jawbones as small as the tip of your finger."

Terrence stopped digging and looked up. "How do you know they're bones, then?"

"We've been doing this a long time and have learned what to look for," Rich answered. He pulled out a small sack from his pocket and took out a set of clear plastic hand lenses. He held one up to his eye. "It's amazing how much better you can see with these things. Use this if you want to examine something up close," Rich said, handing a lens to Terrence.

"Since Terrence found one tooth down here already, there's a good chance there are more fossils nearby," Allison said. She scanned the hills. "This whole area is part of the soil layer we find dinosaur fossils in. It's a great place to look."

"Let's split up into three groups," Rich suggested. "Allison and Kristy can head upstream just a bit. Terrence and I will pair up and explore the gully on the right side of the stream. Mr. and Mrs. Chang, you can explore the gully on the left side of the stream. We haven't been up here in a couple of years. One never knows what might show up after a flood."

Kristy and Allison sloshed up the muddy streambed. Mr. and Mrs. Chang walked across the stream and up a small canyon. Rich and Terrence climbed the gully heading toward the dinosaur dig site they had visited the day before.

"I'll go up here, Rich," Terrence said. He climbed a few steps up one side of the ravine.

"I'll climb here," Rich answered, heading up the other side of the hill. "Let's stay within sight of each other. And let me know if you find anything."

"OK," Terrence answered.

Terrence stepped into soil that was still soaking wet. With each step, his feet squished deeper into the muddy clay. I wonder if I'm smashing tiny fossils, Terrence thought as he turned to see the mess he made. When he was halfway up the hill, he looked back for Rich.

Rich saw Terrence and waved. "It's hard to walk in this mud, isn't it?"

"Yup. Look at the gigantic tracks I just made," Terrence called back. "Maybe they'll fossilize and still be here in a million years!"

Rich smiled. "You never know," he said.

Terrence climbed a bit farther and came to a

bunch of large, sandy rocks, which were easier to walk on. Terrence hopped from rock to rock.

"How's it going up there?" Allison shouted from the streambed.

Terrence turned around. "We haven't found anything yet."

"We haven't, either," Allison called out. "We're heading downstream now. Let's meet back here in half an hour, OK?"

"Sure," Terrence answered. He checked his watch. It was 9:30. "I've got until 10:00 to discover a fossil," he announced.

"Terrence, you can't expect it to happen that fast," Rich said.

Terrence walked along the rocks and continued searching. He turned a bunch of small rocks over in his hands and used the hand lens to look closely at them. There were rough, sandy rocks and smooth, polished ones. A few had sparkling crystals in them, and others were woven with lacy color patterns. I wish I knew what was in all these rocks, he thought.

Terrence continued searching. He inspected more rocks and put each one back where he found it. He imagined that he was a miner searching for gold. Gold miners never knew which rock would have gold in it, and Terrence wasn't going to let any dinosaur "gold" pass him by. He looked closely at more rocks with the hand lens. One after another, Terrence checked for a dried-sponge look or for the shape of a tooth or bone in the rocks. After a few minutes of searching, Terrence stood up and gazed at the thousands of rocks of all shapes and sizes that were scattered around the hills. "This is impossible!" Terrence shouted.

"Impossible . . . impossible . . . impossible," echoed across the canyon.

"Hey, Terrence!" Rich called. "Any luck?"

Terrence looked across the gully and saw Rich standing on a small bluff.

"No! Nothing!" he called back.

"Me neither," Rich replied.

"It's getting hot," Terrence complained. "Are you ready to head back down?"

"We have a little time left to keep looking," Rich called back.

"OK," Terrence said. He continued to examine rocks, although with less enthusiasm than when he first started.

After a while, Rich said, "We probably should get going. We just have time to check in with the others before you'll need to head back to the Visitor Center. We can come back another time."

Terrence picked up a few small rocks and put them in a pile so he would know where to continue his search when he came back. Then he scrambled down the hill to join Rich.

They walked back to the streambed to meet the others.

"What did you find this time, Terrence?" Kristy asked.

"Nothing," Terrence replied, shaking his head. "All those rocks and not one fossil."

"Don't forget, Terrence, you did find that tooth last night," Rich reminded him. "And remember, some paleontologists search a whole lifetime for a discovery like that. You were very lucky."

"I guess you're right," Terrence agreed, "but I want to see a whole dinosaur."

Rich laughed. "We all do."

"Let's take a quick break," Allison suggested. She pointed to a shady area under a grove of small trees 50 feet away. "How about over there?"

"That sounds good," Mr. Chang agreed, fanning his sweaty face with his hat.

They all walked over and sat down on the large rocks near the trees. Terrence found one of the largest rocks and plopped down. "Dad, are we doing anything tomorrow?" he asked.

"No, I scheduled the rafting trip for today, but after that our time is free for the rest of our trip," Mr. Chang said.

"Finding fossils is more work than I thought it would be," said Terrence.

"Have an energy bar," Allison said as she passed them out to the Changs.

Kristy joked, "Maybe these will give us the strength of a dinosaur!"

"Maybe," Allison laughed, and then took a long sip of water. "You know, it's probably close to 100 degrees now, and since you have a rafting trip to take, it might be best for all of us to call it a day. We'll continue our search this evening. Would you like to join us then?" she asked.

Terrence thought it over and said, "Yup, I think I'll give it another try. I already know where I'm going to look next."

"I'd like to come back this evening, too," Mrs. Chang added. "We don't get to hunt for dinosaur fossils every day."

"I'd like to if Terrence and I get back in time and if I have any energy left," Mr. Chang answered.

"OK. But next time I'm going to find a dinosaur," Terrence decided.

Rich stepped over to the large rock that he had

been staring at, put his backpack down, and took out his water bottle. After a quick drink, he set the bottle on the rock, then stopped.

"Allison?" he called out.

"What?" Allison responded.

"Come over here."

Terrence stood still. "What are you looking at?"

Rich slowly spoke. "Come here and you'll see."

The others gathered around the rock.

Rich looked at the small group that surrounded him. "I think I may have found something."

Chapter 10

Another Piece of the Puzzle

Everyone stared at the large, flat, brownish gray rock.

It seemed ordinary to Terrence. He slid his thumbnail across the side of the rock, easily scraping away small grains. "It's really sandy."

"You're right. It's sandstone," Rich replied. "What else do you notice?"

Terrence looked closely. "You mean this?" Terrence asked, pointing to two faint triangular-shaped patterns on the top of the rock.

Mrs. Chang looked where Terrence pointed. "Aren't those just different minerals in the rock?"

Rich blew the dust off the rock and traced the two large patterns with his finger.

"Yes, I see them!" Mr. Chang said excitedly.

"Do you have any idea what they are?" Rich asked.

"Bones?" Terrence asked.

"Yes. I believe they *are* bones," Rich answered.

Kristy looked at the triangles again. "They don't look like bones."

"Actually, I think they're plates from the back of a *Stegosaurus*," Rich finally explained. "They're made up of very thin bone. It's rare to find them in one piece like this."

From her backpack Allison pulled a field guide of fossils. She thumbed through it and found the page labeled *Stegosaurus*.

Everyone gathered around.

Terrence compared the two patterns on the rock to

the sketch in the book. "I can't believe you found *Stegosaurus* plates!" Terrence said, a bit enviously. "I looked at a million rocks and I didn't find a thing."

"Sometimes that's just how things go," Allison laughed. "You search and search and find nothing. Then you give up, and what you're looking for is right in front of your eyes."

"I think we're starting to get a bigger picture of the dinosaur puzzle here," Rich told everyone. "We have a stray *Allosaurus* tooth and a couple of *Stegosaurus* plates about 50 feet away from the tooth. I wonder what was going on back then?"

"I do, too," Allison added. "But that's what's fun about this job. It's like putting a giant 145-million-year-old jigsaw puzzle back together again."

Rich took another look at the rock with the *Stegosaurus* fossils.

"You sure are good at finding things," Terrence said to Rich.

"Well, I know what to look for, and that takes time to learn. And a little bit of luck doesn't hurt, either!" Rich said.

Rich reached into his backpack and took out a pen and a roll of masking tape. He tore off two pieces of tape and wrote "1" on one piece and "2" on the other. He stuck the pieces of tape next to each *Stegosaurus* plate. Then he pulled out a small notebook and wrote something in it.

"What's that for?" Terrence questioned.

"We have to keep track of the location, description, and condition of all fossils we find," Rich explained. "If our luck continues, we'll find lots of other bones out here." Rich scribbled a few things in his notepad, then put it away. "Maybe we *shouldn't* call it a day, Allison."

"I know *I* don't want to leave," Allison replied. "Let's start mapping out the whole area, starting with our little find right here."

Rich pulled out a hammer and pounded a stake in the ground next to the big rock.

"From here," Allison explained, "we'll rope off the area with red string. That way, when we find a fossil, we'll know exactly where it came from. It's going to take us some time to set all this up. I know you need to leave for your rafting trip now, but how about coming back after dinner to see what we've done?"

"That sounds like a great idea!" Mr. Chang said.

"May I snap a picture before we go?" Mrs. Chang asked, pulling her camera from her backpack. "We're going to have quite a slide show when we get back home."

Chapter 11

The Rafting Trip

"I heard you've already been in the water in the park," one of the rafting guides commented as he handed Terrence a life jacket.

"How did you know?" Terrence asked, surprised.

"Word travels fast around here," the guide said, "but if you go in the water again, this time you'll be wearing one of these." He pointed to the life vest.

"OK, let me tell you a few rules of the boat," the guide said. "First of all, keep your life jacket on and always stay in the boat. I may need you two to paddle through some of the rough spots. We'll practice that in a few minutes.

"Everybody ready over there?" he asked the guides in the other boats.

"Yes!" they shouted back. Their passengers were loaded up and they had already pushed into a calm pool of water in a shallow part of the river.

"Ready to go?" the guide asked Terrence and his father after they put on their life vests.

"We sure are," Mr. Chang replied.

"Help me drag this boat into the water," the guide said.

Mr. Chang and Terrence grabbed a handle on each side of the 12-foot-long rubber raft and walked it into shallow water.

"That's cold!" Mr. Chang exclaimed when the water got up to his knees.

"It's about 50 degrees," the guide said. "It's too cold for me, too, but it feels good when it's really hot out, which hopefully it will be today. Hop in." He held the boat as the Changs stepped inside.

The guide shoved the boat as far as he could into the current of the river and then jumped in. Immediately, the boat was briskly moving downstream, chasing after the two boats ahead of them.

"I'm Eric," the guide announced. "And welcome to the heart of Fossil River National Park—the river. I take it you've all been to the dinosaur quarry, right?"

"Yes" Terrence answered.

"Terrence even found a fossil," Mr. Chang bragged.

"Really?" Eric said. "What was it?"

"I found a fossil of an *Allosaurus* tooth, but Rich found *Stegosaurus* plates," Terrence replied.

"Wow! I've looked all over this park and never found anything," Eric said.

Then he went on. "When we hit the rapids, I want us all to focus on staying in the boat. Grab one of these handles." Eric held on to a handle that was attached to the boat. "And tuck your feet under like this." He put his feet at the bottom of the boat and buried them under one of the seats. "That'll hopefully keep us in the boat. The river's a little higher than it usually is at this time of year because we've had a lot of rain recently, so it might be a little rough.

"But we should be OK. Mostly, it's a calm, beautiful ride and I'll be pointing out some of the scenery along the way. But when the rapids come, be ready. My signal will be, 'Hold on!' When I say that, grab the boat like I told you. Let's practice. Ready? Hold on!

"Good job!" Eric said. "OK, why don't both of you paddle with me downstream and see if we can pick up our speed a bit."

The Changs pushed their paddles through the water until the boat moved into the middle of the swiftly flowing river. Terrence watched as rocks zipped by under the water.

"Now, if anyone does get knocked out of the boat, you need to float on your back. Keep your feet up as you go through any rapids. We'll come by and get you with the boat. Don't panic," Eric instructed.

The rubber raft drifted downstream, deeper into the canyon and around a bend. The canyon walls on either side of the stream got steeper and steeper until they were 1,000 feet high. There were colored bands of rocks embedded throughout the canyon walls.

"Look!" Terrence pointed out the red-gray color of a layer of rock halfway up the canyon. "I wonder if there are any dinosaurs buried up there."

"We'll probably never know," Eric answered. "It would be a hard place to dig."

"Take a look at that!" Mr. Chang called out as the boat whisked by a giant, submerged log.

"It looks like a dinosaur bone!" Terrence proclaimed after looking into the water at the thick trunk of an eroded and polished cottonwood tree.

"It kind of does, doesn't it?" Eric said. "Your imagination can run wild out here. And, speaking of *wild*, can you hear that roar ahead?"

The Changs listened to a faint but growing sound of water churning through rocks as they drifted downstream. "That's our first set of rapids up ahead. We call it 'Jaw-Drop.' See that rock over there? Doesn't it look like a giant dinosaur jaw?"

Terrence and his father stared at the dinosaur-shaped rock formation jutting out over the river.

Eric pointed out the features. "See? There are its eye sockets and its nose. Doesn't that jaw look like it's going to drop into the river at any moment?—which is exactly what we're going to do," Eric shouted. "Hold on!"

The Changs each grabbed a handle and tucked their feet under the seats.

Eric glanced at the rapids. "Whoo-hoo! Here we go!"

Quickly, the boat dipped into a large wave. Down, then up. Down, then up. It splashed through some white water. *Slam!* The boat bounced off a rock and

back into the current.

"Hold on!" Eric yelled while paddling with all his might to get the boat to the center of the river.

The Changs held on tightly. Terrence gazed ahead and saw that the boat was . . .

"Ah!" Terrence screamed. "Here we go!"

The boat leaned far forward and hit the bottom of the waterfall. Water splashed all over the boat.

"Wow!" Terrence exclaimed.

Soon the boat was through the rapids and into calmer water, floating gently along.

"It's always nice to get that first rapid out of the way," Eric beamed.

"There's more of those ahead?" Mr. Chang asked.

"Oh, a few. But you did great," Eric said. "We're coming to the heart of the canyon. The water's calm through here, so it's a great place to enjoy the scenery—and relax a little."

Eric slapped on some sunscreen, then adjusted his sunglasses over his eyes. He leaned back in the boat. "I'll let you two be in charge of the boat in this stretch of water," Eric said as he smiled and stretched out.

Gently, Terrence and Mr. Chang dipped and lowered their paddles and steered the raft through the water. The boat glided forward through the calm waters of the canyon.

"It sure is quiet here," Terrence said.

"And relaxing," Mr. Chang said, then yawned.

The boat turned another bend in the river. Up ahead, several boats were parked on a large sandbar. A group of people were hauling large crates into the boats. One by one, the wooden boxes were passed from person to person. The last person carefully placed each heavy box into the boat, making sure it was balanced.

Terrence stopped paddling. "I wonder what they're doing."

As their boat slowly floated past, one of the crew members waved to the Changs. "How ya'll doing?"

"Fine," Terrence answered.

Eric sat up and waved at the people on shore. "They're packing up dinosaur bones and hauling them back to the lab."

"Really?" Terrence asked.

"Yup. There aren't any roads out here. The only way in and out of this canyon is on the river. They come down for a load of boxes every day. See the side canyon up there?" Eric pointed to an opening in the canyon walls on one side of the river. "The story goes that one of our paleontologists was certain that dinosaurs fossils were buried up there. He kept checking over and over. For years he searched the canyon up and down. Other people came with him, but they gave up. Well, one day, he decided to hike up there after a storm—and there you have it. He found skulls, dinosaur backbones—you name it. It's one of the best finds in the park so far."

The boat turned another corner, and they heard a loud, rumbling noise.

The Changs sat up.

"That's right. Time to get ready. Up ahead is a bunch of rapids we call 'Plunge Pool.' Is everyone hanging on?" Eric asked. "Here we go!"

The boat quickly moved into swifter water. It dipped up and down as it gained speed. Up ahead, large waves and white water appeared where the river cascaded over a series of rocks into a large pool.

"Hold on, everyone!" Eric commanded while guiding the boat toward the rapids with his oars.

Terrence and Mr. Chang already had their feet in place and were grasping the boat's handles with all their strength.

"Maybe we shouldn't have taken this rafting trip!" Mr. Chang said as the boat continued gaining speed.

"This is fun, Dad!" Terrence called out. He gazed at where the river was going to take them next. "Is that 'Plunge Pool?'" He pointed ahead as he looked at Eric.

"You bet. Now, hold on tight!" Eric called out. "Whoo-hoo!"

Quickly, the boat plunged into the churning cascades. It slammed into a rock, then bounced back into the current. From there, it took a large dip into a wave and whisked up the other side. It hit an underwater rock and spun around on its side. Water poured into the boat and splashed all over the Changs. Terrence shook his face and blinked his eyes while looking ahead to see what was next.

"Ahh!" Terrence screamed, just as the boat rolled forward over rocks and small waterfalls.

Slam! The boat slammed into a large rock, knocking everyone in the boat forward.

Mr. Chang lost his grip. He sprawled into the front part of the boat, then tried to sit up and move back to his seat.

BAM! The boat hit another rock. Mr. Chang flew into the air and landed in the river.

Terrence jumped out of his seat and screamed, "Dad!"

Eric held out his paddle and said, "Sit down and hold on!"

Terrence's heart pounded as the boat rolled through more rapids.

Mr. Chang kept his feet up and floated through the cascades and into Plunge Pool. For a few seconds, he was pushed underwater by the series of small waterfalls.

Terrence and Eric looked at the river and held their breath as the boat continued tumbling through the rapids. Mr. Chang's head popped up in the calmer waters in the middle of the pool. He shook water from his head and rubbed his eyes as he floated in the water.

Once past the small waterfall, Eric quickly paddled the boat toward Mr. Chang, and then he held out his hand.

"Dad!" Terrence called out as his father slowly dog-paddled to Terrence's side of the boat.

"It's hard to swim in this life jacket," he sputtered

as he grabbed Eric's hand and hoisted himself up the side of the boat. Eric pulled and Terrence grabbed on to his father's life jacket and helped pull him in. Mr. Chang fell into the boat, sat up, and took his seat.

"Boy, that's cold!" he exclaimed. "I don't know how you could stand it yesterday, Terrence."

"Well, that was pretty good timing for a swim," Eric said, smiling. "We get out just ahead. There's a sunny sandbar and snacks for all of you. By the way, Mr. Chang, you did a nice job of floating on your back through the rapids."

Mr. Chang smiled. "Thanks, but I wouldn't want to do it again."

Eric paddled the boat toward the beach. Other boats had already landed there and a picnic table had been set up. Guides were placing plates of fruit and other snacks on the big table.

Eric stepped out of the boat and tugged it into shallow waters. "Welcome to Stegosaurus Beach!" he proclaimed. "The bus will pick you up here in about 30 minutes. Until then, help yourself to some food. You can swim here, too, if you want."

Mr. Chang and Terrence laughed. "I think we've had enough swimming for this trip."

Eric smiled. "You can drop off your life jackets in

that pile over there. And, sir, if you want, you can hang your wet shirt up to dry on that clothesline."

Eric hauled the boat up the beach while Terrence and Mr. Chang walked over to one of the tables and sat down, happy to be on solid ground again.

Chapter 12

Back at the Dig

Early in the evening, Mr. Chang and Terrence met Mrs. Chang and Kristy back at the campsite and then they all drove to the now-familiar parking area near the fossil site. Allison and Rich's trucks were still parked there.

There was a new sign at the trailhead.

CAUTION

Trail Closed Until Further Notice

Terrence pointed to the ground. "Look at all the footprints."

"It looks like Rich and Allison brought a wheelbarrow up here," Mr. Chang added, pointing to the tire tracks going up the center of the path.

"This won't be a faint trail much longer," Mrs. Chang remarked.

Terrence started walking faster. "Not if they keep finding dinosaur fossils in here!"

He was the first to reach the dig site. Terrence ran

across the stream to find Allison and Rich. He stopped and looked at the rock with the *Stegosaurus* plates. Piles of dirt were scooped out around it, but the plates were still in place.

Next to the rock was the stake Allison had put in earlier. From that point, a line of red string outlined the whole area. Scattered around the dig site were picks, shovels, and several large buckets filled with rocks.

"Rich and Allison sure have been busy," Mrs. Chang said, "but I wonder where they are."

"Listen!" Kristy exclaimed. She pointed uphill.

Allison appeared from behind some small trees, pushing a wheelbarrow full of rocks. "There you guys are! We were hoping you'd come back."

"Did you find anything else?" Terrence asked.

"I can hardly believe it myself," Allison beamed. She set the wheelbarrow down and wiped her dusty face with her arm. I searched all around this area a few years ago. And I've hunted for fossils throughout the park. We've found dinosaur fossils before, but it's rare to discover so many in one area. You should see what's around here. We've found rib bones, legs, vertebrae, and several more *Stegosaurus* plates. There are plenty of other bones we can't identify. Take a look at the rocks in these buckets."

Terrence grabbed one and held it up. Embedded in it was a grayish bone material that had a dry, spongy look.

"Is this a fossil?" Terrence asked.

"You bet," Allison answered. "It's part of a rib bone."

"This whole hillside is one big fossil gold mine," Rich said, coming down the trail carrying two buckets loaded with rocks. He set the buckets down next to the wheelbarrow and took out a large, uneven rock the size of a football. "Come see what I have."

Allison and the Changs gathered around. He turned the rock over.

"It's another *Allosaurus* tooth," Terrence exclaimed. "Another lucky strike!"

"We've never had so much luck in such a short period of time," Allison stated.

"And we may never again," Rich added. "For us paleontologists, this is as good as it gets."

"What are you going to do with all these rocks and fossils?" Mr. Chang asked.

"We'll haul them all out," Rich explained, "but that could take months."

"And then what?" Mrs. Chang asked.

"We'll take them to the lab," Allison replied. "That's where the fun really starts!"

"The dig site is just the beginning of our work," Rich explained. "We have volunteers back in the lab who separate the fossils from the rock. Then we try to identify them and match them with other fossils. If there are enough bones, we can sometimes put parts of dinosaurs, like skulls or feet, back together. In rare cases, we might even be able to piece together a full skeleton."

"That's the most exciting part of our work," Allison said.

"All of this takes a lot of time," Rich added. "Volunteers work all year long in the lab. We work outside on dig sites only in the summer."

Terrence looked disappointed. "You mean you aren't out here every day? When I'm a paleontologist, I want to be out digging all the time."

Allison laughed. "We do a lot of our testing in the lab in the winter months. If you're a paleontologist, you'll always have plenty of work to do."

"Let's get back to the work we're doing right now," Rich said. "You know, even with all that we've found, I'm sure there are more bones out here."

"Can I look around some more?" Terrence asked.

"Of course," Allison answered. "This gully seems to be a good place to look."

Terrence looked at his parents. "Can I go back up

the hill where I left off earlier, Mom and Dad?"

"Sure," Mr. Chang replied. "I'll keep looking up the other side."

Another search for dinosaur fossils began.

Chapter 13

Persistence

Terrence hiked up the same side of the hill he had climbed earlier in the day. He looked over and saw his father on the other side of the gully. Terrence found the small pile of rocks he had left and climbed toward them.

He looked all over the hillside at the hundreds of rocks of all shapes and sizes that were scattered about. Terrence thought about the people who discovered the bones in the park back in 1906. People had searched the canyon for years before they found anything, and many of them had been scientists. Terrence remembered Rich's words—*Some paleontologists search an entire lifetime . . .*

"I don't *have* an entire lifetime!" Terrence yelled. "We're going home tomorrow!"

"What about tomorrow?" Terrence's father called from across the way. "You know we have to leave early in the morning."

"I know, Dad," Terrence replied. "I was just thinking out loud."

Terrence wished he had the keen eyesight of an eagle. He would be able to spot even tiny things, like miniature fossils.

Terrence's eager eyes searched the hills. He thought about what had been found so far: an *Allosaurus* tooth in the stream, some *Stegosaurus* plates nearby, another *Allosaurus* tooth farther up the hill, and some scattered bones lying around.

"There's got to be a bigger clue to the puzzle somewhere around here," Terrence decided.

He walked past his small pile of rocks and zig-zagged back and forth along the hillside. Terrence concentrated harder than he had ever concentrated on anything. Back and forth he went, covering every inch of ground, just like he did when he was at home mowing his lawn. Every piece of ground was going to be inspected. Just as he left no patch of grass uncut, he would leave no stone unturned.

Terrence stared at the ground as he walked slowly uphill. He bent down and inspected a small rock, pulled out his hand lens, and peered at it closely. He turned it over and over. Nothing on it looked like a bone.

Once he was low to the ground, Terrence realized it was much easier to look for tiny clues. He crawled along the ground, looking at all the rocks in his path.

No stone unturned . . . it took him years. The words continued to ring in Terrence's head. Another word— *persistence*—came to mind. Terrence's dad used that word when Terrence wanted to give up on his science fair project.

For a moment, Terrence stopped and stood up. He looked across the way at his father, who was walking on the other side of the gully, looking at the ground. Terrence glanced down the canyon toward the dig site that Rich and Allison had set up. He noticed that Allison was lighting a lantern for the evening search. Terrence gazed up and realized that the sun had started to set. The first stars of the evening were starting to twinkle, and the sky was fading to soft purple.

Terrence looked to the east and saw Split Mountain imitating the colors of the sunset and fading to a pink glow. A gentle breeze touched his face. The air had cooled.

"Terrence," his dad called, "it's getting dark. Let's head back down now."

"Can I look for a few more minutes, Dad?" Terrence pleaded.

"We've already been up here for over an hour," Mr. Chang said. He saw that Terrence had already started searching again. Mr. Chang climbed partway down the hill and sat down on a large rock to watch his son.

Because daylight was fading, Terrence quickly paced back and forth along the hill. He picked up one rock after another and turned them over. He inspected large boulders, brushing some off to check for fossils.

"I want to keep looking. I'm not giving up," Terrence said to himself.

"Terrence," his dad called, "come here for a minute."

Terrence saw his dad sitting down on some rocks. Terrence dropped the rock he was holding and walked over to him.

"Sit down," Mr. Chang said. He moved over and let Terrence join him on the rock. "This has been a pretty good vacation, hasn't it?" Mr. Chang asked.

"This has been a *great* vacation," Terrence replied.

"We've had quite an adventure. I guess we both have a new respect for the power of nature—water power especially," his dad said. "And you've seen your share of fossils, haven't you?"

"I'll say," Terrence said.

"Has this trip given you any ideas about your science fair project?" Mr. Chang asked.

"You know what? It's been so much fun learning about fossils that winning a prize for it doesn't seem so important anymore. I was thinking that I might do a project to show everyone what cool jobs paleontologists have."

"Well then, I'm certainly glad we came," Mr. Chang said.

"I don't want to go home yet," Terrence moaned.

"Me neither," Mr. Chang said. "But your mother and I have to get back to work. And you, my son, go back to school next week!"

Terrence sighed. "I know."

Terrence squinted his eyes in the dim light and looked at a large pile of rocks. "Hey," he said, "it's kind of dark, but do you notice anything unusual about those rocks up ahead?"

"No, not really. They just look like rocks to me, just like all the others out here," Mr. Chang said.

Terrence kept staring at the rocks. He jumped up and ran over to get a closer look at the top of a large boulder. Most of it was buried in the ground. Terrence studied the top of it. At first it was hard to see in the growing darkness. He brushed off some loose dirt. Then he blew several times on different parts of the rock to clear it off as much as possible. Terrence looked at the rock again and could barely make out a dark-colored outline. He traced it with his finger, then gulped. It was hard and felt different from the rest of the rock.

"Dad! I think you should come here," Terrence called.

While his father walked over, Terrence touched the embedded shape again. It seemed to cover a large part of the boulder.

Mr. Chang bent down.

"Look, Dad," Terrence said, while pointing to the object. "Doesn't it look like an eye could go here? And in this other hole, an ear?"

Mr. Chang nodded. "Yes, I see what you mean. I wish it were lighter so we could see better." He ran his hand over an oval shape at the bottom. "This sure seems like it could be a jaw."

In the middle of the object was a series of sharp points that were several inches long.

"These could be teeth," Terrence said, "but I think a few are missing."

Terrence and Mr. Chang looked at each other and grinned.

Chapter 14

Terrence's Prize

Terrence and his father heard voices and saw a group of lights moving toward them.

"Here you are," Allison said.

"We've been worried about you!" Mrs. Chang added.

"Yeah, and it's way past my bedtime!" Kristy said gleefully.

"Can I borrow one of those flashlights for a minute?" Terrence managed to ask Allison and Rich.

"Sure," Allison replied. "What is it?"

Terrence took the flashlight from Allison and shined the light on the top of the rock. "Look!"

Everyone gathered around the rock.

"We just noticed this a few minutes ago," Terrence said.

Rich and Allison studied the rock closely.

"Terrence . . ." Rich started to say.

Allison gulped. "I think you've found . . ."

"You guys, wait right here!" Rich said. He grabbed another flashlight and ran off down the trail.

"Where's he going?" Kristy asked.

"I think I have a pretty good idea," Allison answered.

When Rich returned, he announced, "I've got to try this." He took two teeth from a plastic bag and held them over the two gaps in the jaw.

Terrence looked at the two loose teeth. Then he looked at the size, sharpness, and grooves of the teeth still in the skull. He took a closer look with his hand lens. "This is an *Allosaurus* skull!" he exclaimed.

"I think you're right," Allison said. "But we won't be sure until we get the skull out of the ground."

Allison reached down and touched a scar at the front of the skull. "Did you notice this large indentation here? I wonder what happened."

"I have an idea about what might have happened," Rich said. He pulled out a sharp, 2-foot-long, bony-looking rock from his pack. "Allison and I just found this a short while ago near the *Stegosaurus* plates. You know what this is, don't you?"

"I'm not sure," Terrence replied. "Maybe it's a spike from a *Stegosaurus* tail?"

"You bet," Rich stated. "Now check this out." He placed the sharp object right over the large dent in the skull.

"It looks like that spike made that dent," Terrence said.

"So what you're saying," Mr. Chang thought out loud, "is that the *Stegosaurus* we found hit its tail spike against this *Allosaurus* here?"

"Could be," Allison replied.

"Is that how the *Allosaurus* died?" Kristy asked.

Allison shrugged. "We can't be sure, but it does seem like the *Stegosaurus* and *Allosaurus* knew each other."

Terrence took the two teeth from Rich and held

them up. "How did the *Allosaurus* lose these teeth?"

"Who knows?" Allison answered. "The loose teeth could've simply fallen out. Or, perhaps . . ."

Allison thought for a while before she began her story. "Picture this stream 145 million years ago," Allison said. "It was a river then, surrounded by a hot, humid forest. Suddenly the ground starts to vibrate. *BOOM! BOOM! BOOM!* A *Stegosaurus* walks toward the edge of the river, takes a drink, and then splashes into the river."

Allison continued. "Then the wind picks up and begins whooshing through the trees. Lightning flashes and thunder rumbles. The air becomes still and it begins to rain."

Allison paused for a moment, then said, "As the rain hits the ground, a hungry *Allosaurus* thrashes through the forest, searching for a meal. When the *Allosaurus* reaches the river, it sees the *Stegosaurus.*"

"Then what happened?" asked Kristy.

"Shhh," Terrence said.

"The *Allosaurus* steps into the river. Lightning flickers and the rain turns into a heavy downpour. The *Allosaurus* tromps through the water. When it gets close to the *Stegosaurus,* it roars, baring its sharp teeth."

As Allison spoke, Terrence glanced at the *Allosaurus* skull in the rock.

Allison went on, "The *Stegosaurus* frantically wades toward shore. The river is now muddy and deep and starts to flow rapidly. The *Stegosaurus* tries to get away but its feet become stuck in the mud on the river bottom."

"Poor *Stegosaurus*," Kristy interrupted.

Allison smiled at Kristy before she continued. "Quickly, the *Allosaurus* closes in on the *Stegosaurus*. Its jaws snap through several of the *Stegosaurus*' plates. The plates drop into the river and swirl downstream."

"Mean *Allosaurus*," Kristy added, as everyone's eyes went to the jaws in the *Allosaurus* skull.

"The *Stegosaurus* pries its feet loose from the mud and slaps its sharp tail spikes against the *Allosaurus*, knocking one of its teeth loose. The tooth flies through the air, lands on the water, and sinks. The *Allosaurus* chomps on the *Stegosaurus*' neck. The *Stegosaurus* shakes free but it loses its balance and is swept off its feet and down the river."

"Wow! Then what?" asked Terrence.

"Shhh," said Kristy.

"*ZAP!* Lightning strikes the *Allosaurus*' head. The *Allosaurus* topples over and is swept into the current.

Its body is pulled downstream into deeper waters along with the *Stegosaurus.* The river has now swelled to a huge lake. And our dinosaurs lie buried at the bottom of the muddy lake."

"Do you really think that's what happened?" Terrence asked.

"Maybe. We need more information to support my guess and we probably will never know for sure," replied Allison, "but that's what makes our job so interesting."

Rich picked up the lantern and gazed around the area. "I wonder what else is buried nearby."

"Would you like to join us for some more dinosaur digging tomorrow?" Allison asked the Changs.

"Of course we would, but . . ." Mrs. Chang answered.

Terrence's heart skipped a beat. He thought for a moment that his parents were going to extend their vacation.

Mrs. Chang went on, "We have a long day ahead of us, and it's back to work for us—and school for the kids."

"Oh well," Terrence muttered.

"Well, we know exactly where we're going to start another excavation first thing in the morning!" Rich spoke. "We've got a lot to do out here."

"You know, there's something we should tell you, Terrence," Allison said. "When someone discovers dinosaur bones, the dig site is named after that person."

Rich nodded. "That's right! We're going to call this place 'The Terrence Chang Site.'"

Terrence's eyes lit up. "Really? You'll name it after me?"

"Absolutely!" Rich and Allison said together.

Mrs. Chang put her arm around her son. "That's really exciting, Terrence."

Mr. Chang patted Terrence on the back.

"I guess we have to say good-bye now," Mrs. Chang said slowly. She turned to Allison and Rich. "It sure has been great meeting both of you and learning all about dinosaurs and fossils."

Rich shook hands with the Changs. "We're glad we got to know each of you."

"I hope you do become a paleontologist someday," Allison added as she put a hand on Terrence's shoulder.

"I'm glad I got to help you," Terrence said to Allison and Rich.

"Good-bye," Kristy called out. "Take care of the dinosaurs."

"We will, Kristy," Allison answered.

"You can use our flashlights as you hike out," said Rich, handing the light to Mrs. Chang, "Just leave them in the truck."

The Changs started heading up the trail to the parking lot. Mrs. Chang turned on one flashlight and Terrence flicked on the other. The Changs walked up the trail, with Terrence lagging behind.

He stood gazing up at the stars. He saw the shapes of dinosaur teeth in the nighttime sky. "Look!" he said, not realizing his family was too far ahead to hear.

Terrence heard some clanging and banging where Allison and Rich were. He turned around and saw Allison and Rich putting away tools in the yellow glow of the lantern light.

They saw Terrence and waved.

"We'll write to you and let you know how the excavation is going," Rich called out.

"And we'll send you pictures of the fossils we find, too," Allison added.

"Thanks!" Terrence replied. He waved to Rich and Allison, then turned and jogged up the trail toward his family.

When he caught up to them, he began singing, *"We're going hiking, hiking, hiking. We're going hiking by the stream!"*